Paula's Feeling Angry

written by Melanie Aldridge
illustrated by Peg Roth Haag

To the teacher or parent:

This book deals with both anger and jealousy. Paula Jean is jealous of her baby brother and angry over the attention her mother pays to him. These are feelings many young children have. In the story, Paula Jean's mother sets firm limits to her daughter's behavior, while at the same time understanding Paula Jean's need for love and attention. Then, the mother begins to help Paula Jean see how both she and Baby Carl fit into the family.

All preschool children need this kind of help. They need acceptance as lovable people, along with limitations on unacceptable behavior.

As children grow, they can begin to understand that they themselves hold the responsibility for their actions. Then it is time to teach them ways to deal with negative attitudes and feelings.

Teach children that prayer is an important aid in overcoming anger and jealousy. God has promised His help. Prayer is an avenue by which we receive His help.

Use this book to introduce discussion. Here are some questions you might ask. 1. How did Paula Jean feel about her baby brother? 2. Have you ever felt this way? Tell me about it. 3. How did Paula Jean get over being angry? 4. How did her mother help her? 5. What does Jesus say about how we should treat each other? 6. How did Jesus treat people?

THE CHILD'S WORLD

ELGIN, ILLINOIS 60120

Paula Jean was feeling angry.
She didn't know why.
It couldn't have been
because of the new baby,
Baby Carl.
Oh no, it couldn't.
Paula Jean was just feeling angry.

Distributed by Standard Publishing, 8121
Hamilton Avenue, Cincinnati, Ohio 45231.

Library of Congress Cataloging in Publication Data

Paula's feeling angry.

(A Values series)
Published in 1976 under title: Feeling angry.
SUMMARY: Paula Jean feels angry because her mother
pays so much attention to her new baby brother.
[1. Anger—Fiction.   2. Brothers and sisters—
Fiction.   3. Babies—Fiction.   4. Christian life—
Fiction]   I. Haag, Peg Roth.   II. Title.   III. Series.
PZ7.T288Pau 1979   [E]   79-10773
ISBN 0-89565-076-2

"I know," said Paula Jean.
"I'll send him away,
far, far away.
Then Momma can rock me.
Momma will be happy, rocking me."

But somehow that made Paula Jean feel worse,
angry and scared all together.
Paula Jean ran to the crib to check.
The baby was still there,
stretching in his sleep.
Of course he was still there.
Pretend only happens when people are pretending.
It's never for real.

Paula Jean reached in and patted his head.
She was still feeling angry.
She touched his fingers,
then pinched them . . . hard!
And the baby cried out.
He cried and cried.
Of course he did.
When people pinch for real,
it hurts for real.

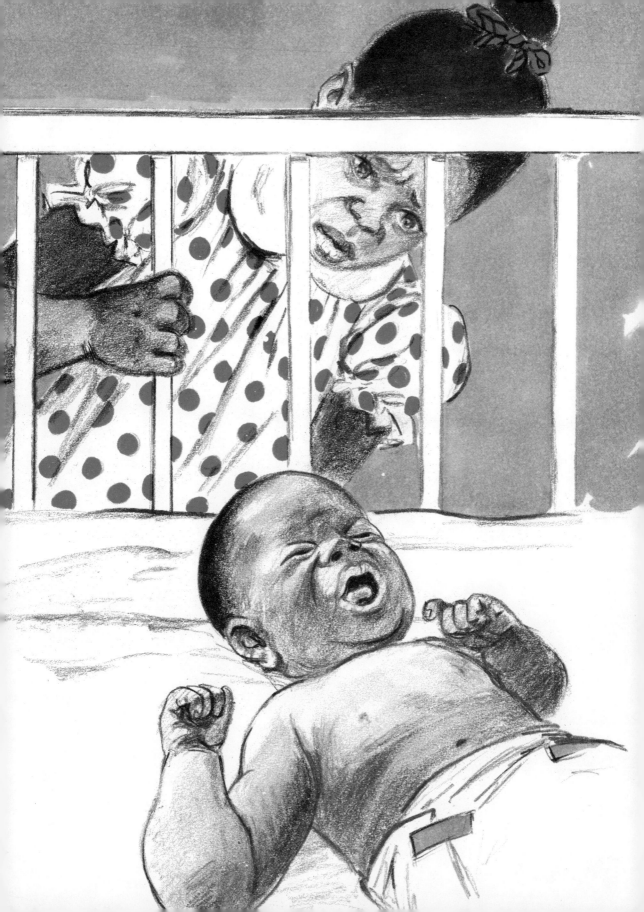

Now Paula Jean really felt bad,
angry and scared, oh, so scared.
''Momma!'' she called. ''Come quick!
Baby Carl is crying.
I didn't do it! Really I didn't!
Make him stop crying right now!''

11

Momma came,
and Momma picked up Baby Carl.
Momma soothed and hushed
and gentled Baby Carl.
He stopped crying
and went right back
to sleep.

"Now then," said Momma to Paula Jean,
"tell me what's been happening."

"I didn't make him cry," said Paula Jean.
"I only patted his head. Really I did.
I didn't pinch him or anything."

"I see," said Momma. "Are you sure?"

Paula Jean looked down at the floor.
"Well . . ." Paula Jean said, then stopped.

"Come sit with me," said Momma.
They rocked and rocked.
"We don't allow pinching," Momma said.
"Not ever.
We don't let people pinch you,
and we don't let you pinch people.
Jesus taught us to love each other
and not to hurt each other.
Let's ask Him to help you love Baby Carl
and not want to hurt him."
And they did.

"I'm sorry," said Paula Jean.
"I won't pinch. Not ever again."

"That's my girl," said Momma.
"That's my big, good girl."

Paula Jean felt much better.
For a while.
But when Momma had to bathe Baby Carl,
Paula Jean felt angry again,
angry and very lonely.
So she pounded with her hammer set.
She pounded and pounded and pounded.
As Paula Jean pounded,
she remembered what her mother had said
about Jesus.
She remembered her mother's prayer.
Paula Jean pounded a little more,
slower and slower.
Then she didn't need to pound anymore.

"Can I taste Baby Carl's milk?" asked Paula Jean.

"Oh, I guess so," said Momma,
giving Paula Jean another bottle.

Paula Jean sat down in a corner
and sucked on the bottle.
The milk was warm,
not cold like milk from a glass.
And it tasted funny,
not good like milk from a glass.
Paula Jean took the bottle back to her mother.

"Why do you make him drink that stuff?"
she asked. "It tastes terrible."

Momma laughed.
"Climb up here beside me," she said,
"and we'll feed Baby Carl together."
Paula Jean settled down,
warm and close, by her mother.
"Many babies like warm milk," said Momma.
"You liked warm milk when you were a baby."

"Did you rock me and feed me,
just like Baby Carl?" asked Paula Jean.

"I sure did.
Just like Baby Carl.
And I bathed you and dressed you,
just like Baby Carl.
And I changed your diapers,
just like Baby Carl."

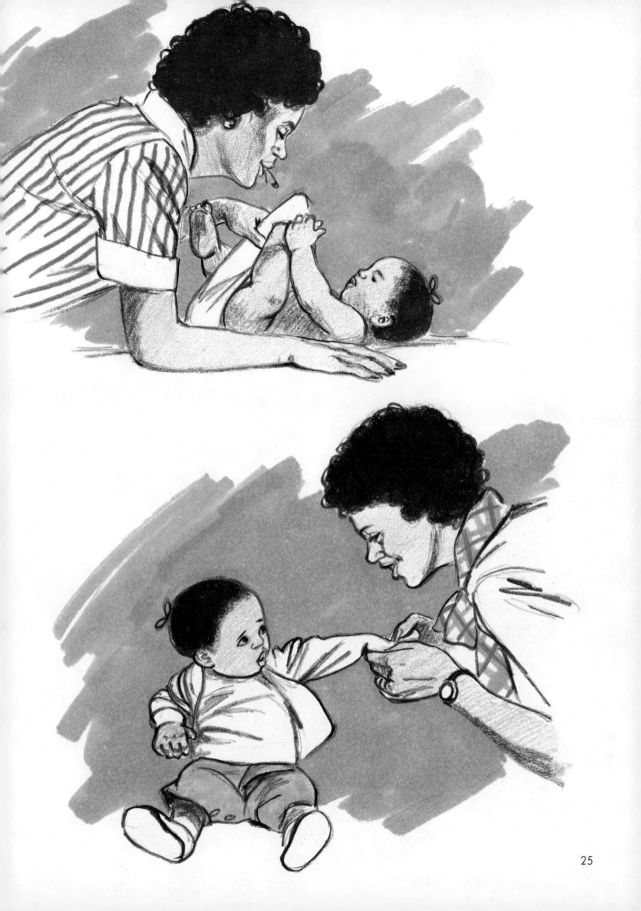

"What was I like when I was a baby?"
asked Paula Jean.

"Oh, you were beautiful.
Such curly black hair you had, so soft!
Such beautiful brown skin you had!
Such big brown eyes you had!
And you were always reaching out,
always grabbing things,
always putting things in your mouth
to see how they tasted.

"At church, you always grabbed for the
pencils in back of the pews.
And every time Daddy picked you up,
you grabbed the pen in his pocket."
Momma laughed. "Daddy used to say
you were the 'grabbingest' baby he'd ever seen."

"Did he really?" asked Paula Jean.

"Yes, he did. He was very proud of you.
He said it showed you were curious.'
You still are, you know. Very curious."

29

"Is Baby Carl a grabber?" asked Paula Jean.

Momma smiled. "Not yet.
Baby Carl is a stretcher.
See him stretch?"

"Can I hold him?" asked Paula Jean.

"Ahh, you're still a grabber," said Momma,
smiling down at her.
She showed Paula Jean just how to hold her arms.
Then she placed Baby Carl just so.

"My two beautiful children," said Momma.
And somehow, Paula Jean didn't feel angry at all.

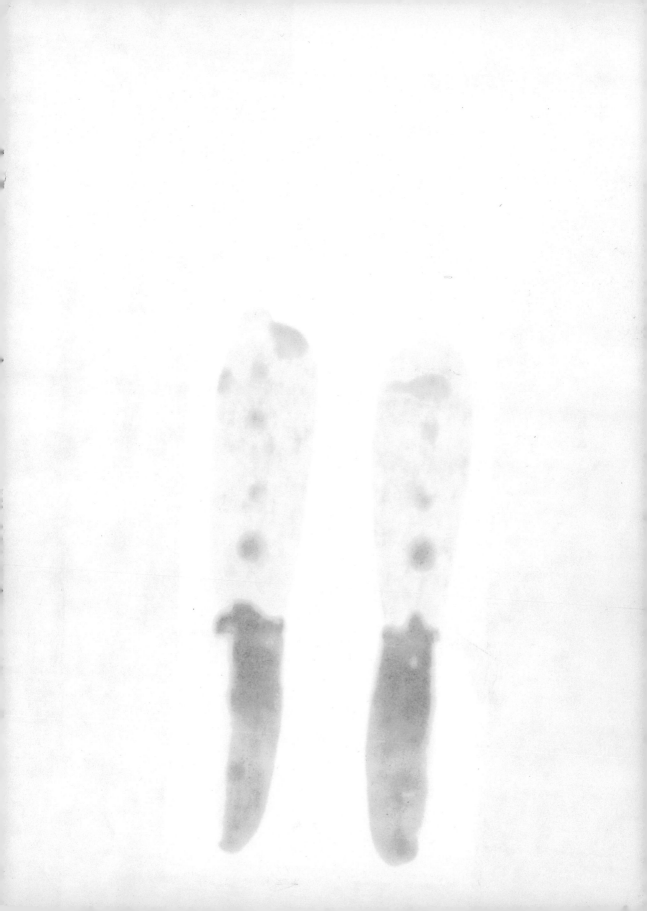

JUV CPH AUDRIDGE MELANIE
Audridge, Melanie
Paula's feeling angry

Date Due

MAY 2 0 1980	APR 2 6 1994		
MAY 2 0 1980			
OCT 2 3 1980	MAY 1 2 1995		
OCT 2 3 1980			
DEC 0 2 1980			
DEC 0 2 1980			
APR 2 7 1982			
SEP 2 0 1983			
MAY 8 1984			
MAY	SEP 2 5 2000		
MAR 1			

Concordia College Library
Bronxville, NY   10708